GEMINI
ERROR

A. D. Phillips

ISBN: 1481830570
ISBN-13: 978-1481830577

DEDICATION

I dedicate this book, to everyone that told me that I could, when I was not so sure myself. Thanks for the boost.

CONTENTS

ACKNOWLEDGMENTS

First, I would like to say thank you to all of the people that supported me and spoke blessings of prosperity into my life. It is because of you, that I decided to revise this short tale. Enjoy. ☺ (P.S., I really did enjoy revisiting one of my favorite rough drafts, and giving it new life. It is a rather excellent story.)

Prelude
Introduction to error

INSIDE the home of Mr. and Mrs. Struthers, an intense argument is ensuing. Mrs. Struthers has just arrived home after staying out all night with her friends. The tension in the air is at suffocating levels.

"I told you me and my girlfriends Trisha and Alicia just had a night out on the town! I got too drunk, and I ended up sleeping in Alicia's guest room. That's all, I promise you!" Amanda protests as her husband hurls accusations at her. She has a pounding headache from the night before, and her outer appearance clearly shows evidence of a night of debauchery. Her long, jet-black hair is tangled and matted with a mixture of hair products, sweat, and naturally produced oils, red faded, smeared lipstick covers her soft pouty lips. Her light brown skin is sticky with old sweat. The cheeks on her face have a slight tinge of red. The smell of alcohol is still detectable on her breath. Her tight exposing dress, is something that a married woman has no business even thinking about purchasing, let alone wearing.

"Look, I know something's going on so don't try to make me think otherwise! That's like saying shit don't stink!" Mr. Struthers yells furiously as spittle shoots out of his now foaming mouth. He knows that something isn't right. He smells the faint scent of cologne mixed in with the overbearing stench of alcohol on her. His disheveled appearance, his brown thinning mess of hair is wildly unattractive; he reeks of cigarettes, weed, and days of not bathing. His dingy wife beater hangs and is slightly stretched out from repeated wear. "Oh, and I guess Alicia sprays her guest room bedding with cologne huh?" Even through his smoke scent filled nostrils, he knows when he smells a masculine scent.

"See there you go with that shit again! You're always getting so mad and riled up over nothing! You need anger management! I hate when you get that crazy look in your eyes and start foaming at the mouth!"

"Oh so now I need anger management cause my wife's out fucking some joker behind my back! Mandy I know something ain't right, your friends can't cover for you forever!"

"I told you that I don't like being called Mandy, it sounds too white, and if you want to believe that you're married to a hoe, then you might as well not be with me! I told you it wasn't going to happen again! I make one little mistake, and I end up paying for it for the rest of my life! You had a choice to leave, or forgive me and work it out! You chose to work it out! What you need to do is get over your insecurity trip, cause I'm not the problem!" With that being said, Amanda leaves the room, Carl contemplates following her, and continuing until he feels satisfied, but after staying up practically the whole night waiting for her to come home, he doesn't have the strength to carry on. He just lets it go. "I guess I shouldn't have dated outside of my race." He mumbles as he thinks back to one of the last conversations that he had with his old man before they fell out. His remembers his father telling him that if he chose to be with Amanda Perez, then he was no longer a part of their family. He can just hear his father saying, "I told you so".

In another part of the house, Amanda's guilt is getting the best of her. She doesn't have the heart to tell him the truth. She knows that it will hurt him even more than the first time. She wonders if she should just file for divorce and spare his already broken pride and shattered feelings. Legally, it would probably be in her best interest not to tell him. She can simply say she wants a divorce due to negligence of husbandly duties. Even before she crossed the line and strayed outside of the marriage for the second time, he was already accusing her of cheating, even more so, after he was laid-off. In some weird twisted way, his accusations pushed her away, and into the arms of another man. She knows that he really doesn't deserve what she's doing to him. He deserves so much better than this. Amanda goes into the bathroom, locks the door, falls to her knees, and starts to sob uncontrollably; this is definitely, not the way that she intended to spend the morning after a great night.

Meanwhile, inside of the office of attorney Arnold Spellman, private investigator Malcolm Scott sits with the attorney as he discusses his current case. Arnold Spellman has features that are very Morris Chestnut-esque, his dark smooth creaseless skin, tender eyes, handsome smile, and stature, make many women long to be Mrs. Spellman. Arnold Spellman is one of the highest regarded black attorneys in the city, and even though he hates the label "one of the city's best black attorneys", he accepts the acknowledgement never the less. He hates living in a world that is so fixated on class and color, mainly the latter. No matter how much he excels, or how many honors he achieves, his color is always the first thing that most notice.

"Mr. Scott, I need you to gather as much evidence as possible on the extramarital activities of my client's husband, Harold Atkins." Mr. Spellman says as he lays a yellow envelope on the desk in front of him. "I need to build a strong enough case against the guy. So much so to the point that; the judge doesn't even want to hear two words from him. I need concrete, irrefutable proof, and I need it within a timely manner, how soon can you have it ready?" Mr. Spellman expresses while maintaining eye contact with the bleach blond, blue-eyed detective. Malcolm Scott is a person that people often describe as someone that doesn't live up to their full potential. With his handsome boyish looks, he could've easily been a heartthrob having his fair share of women, but he chose to pursue his childhood dream instead. He was always a big crime show buff. As a child, he would watch reruns of "Magnum P.I.", "Remington Steele", and "Murder she wrote". Even with the few extra pounds that he's managed to put on over the years, he is still a rather attractive specimen.

"Umm give me a few days and let me see what I can put together. I should have all of the evidence you need within a week's time." Malcolm responds as he opens up the yellow envelope and looks through its contents. He takes out a picture of Harold. While he studies the picture of the pitiful excuse of a man, attorney Spellman takes out his checkbook, writes out a check and gives it to him.

"I will contact you by the end of this week and let you know what I have." Malcolm says before leaving the attorney's office with the check and yellow envelope in hand. As he walks down the hall, Malcolm continues to stare at the picture. He hates men like Harold. He believes that its guys like him that makes it hard for good guys. Men like Harold, are also the reason why Malcolm loves his job. He loves helping expose two timing losers.

Later that day, while Harold Atkins is at work, his wife Denise Atkins receives a call from attorney Spellman.

"Hello Denise, this is attorney Spellman. I was just calling to inform you that I've found a way to get the evidence we need against your husband, but I'm going to need you to help me out."

"Okay sure, what else do you need?"

"Well for starters, I'm going to need access to your husband's cell phone account, and I'm also going to need you to enable the GPS tracking function on his phone. Plus, it would also be helpful if you gave us a list of all of his friends and acquaintances."

"Alright, it might take a few days, but I'm sure that I can get all of that handled. So once it's all done, how long do you think it will take to get some substantial evidence?"

"Umm it should take no more than two weeks tops to compile enough evidence to get the ball rolling. I already have someone working on it as we speak. He's a real straight shooter, so I know he will get us exactly what we need. Trust me; we're going to get you everything that you deserve Mrs. Atkins."

"Thank you Mr. Spellman."

"You're welcome. I will be in touch" Attorney Spellman

finishes the conversation, and quickly dials up P. I. Scott. Mr. Scott is in the middle of eating when he picks up the phone.

"Hey Mr. Spellman, what can I help you with?" He asks in a garbled tone in between bites of food.

"Hey Malcolm, I have some more things that might make your job easier…"

DAY 1

12:05pm: Amanda pulls up to Harold's company. As she exits her vehicle, Harold greets her. Harold fits the tall dark and handsome label to a tee. His olive toned skin, dark hair with slight sprinkles of gray, chiseled facial features, cool grayish blue eyes, and muscular toned frame, make it hard for the opposite sex to shy away from him. Harold places a quick peck on her cheek as they embrace. They then get in her car, and proceed to their destination.

"I had a great time the other night," Amanda says while keeping her eyes focused on the road.

"I did too. I'm glad that I was able to get you for a whole night. It was awesome!" Harold responds as he reminisces

"So be honest, do you have anybody else?" Amanda asks and hopes that Harold responds exactly how she envisions in her head.

"Why should it matter, you're still married, and you obliviously know that I'm married, so If I did have another girl or two, it wouldn't matter because we're not in a committed relationship." Harold's answer is bitter but true. It has definitely burst Amanda's bubble, but it is what it is, and if she wants to be with him, she has no choice but to accept it.

12:18pm: The couple arrives at one of Harold's favorite restaurants, Toni's. Toni's is an upscale eatery on the eastside of town. The city's social elite frequent it. Its exclusivity is what keeps them coming back. Lost in a moment of passion, Harold places a very intimate kiss on Amanda's lips before they exit the vehicle. Unbeknownst to Harold, every detail of the kiss; is being recorded. Malcolm has been following them since they left Harold's office. Harold and Amanda exit her vehicle. Preoccupied with the lust and excitement of the moment, both are oblivious to everything else around them. Malcolm watches them walk into the restaurant holding hands. He snaps a quick series of photos. He makes sure to get as many pictures within those few seconds as possible. He wants to follow them inside and get juicier footage, but he knows that it would go against one of his sacred rules, and that is, never get too close to the subject. Malcolm resists his urge and stays in the car to avoid detection.

Once inside the restaurant, an atmosphere of class surrounds Harold and Amanda. The walls of the restaurant are a deep wine color with subtle dark chocolate wood accents. The lighting is flawlessly set to suit the relaxed contemporary environment. Plush private booths line the walls. Circular shaped glass tables, trimmed with classy dark polished wood, occupy the space in the main dining area. As surprising as it is, this is Amanda's first time at Toni's. She takes it all in as they approach the host of the restaurant. The host is a husky mulatto man named James. He has seen Harold come in on so many different occasions, in the company of so many different women, that it sickens him. He sees the light brown Latina beauty, and envy instantly sets in. Her long dark hair perfectly accentuates her facial features. Her slim but curvy frame screams for attention. James can't stand Harold. If it were not for the fact that Harold is good friends with the restaurant's owner, James would have done everything in his power to expose him ages ago. Deep down, James despises guys like Harold. He feels that its people like Harold that get everything in life (including an abundance of women), and leaves scraps and broken hearts for men like himself to deal with. James has memorized Harold's favorite dishes. Every time he orders any of them, James makes sure to add a little something extra to them as his way of winning one for the "little guys".

"Hello, welcome to Toni's, my name is James, how may I help you today?" James hates having to force himself to say that line every time Harold visits with a new piece of meat on his arm. He hates it, but does it for the sake of keeping his job, and receiving a more than generous tip at the end of each visit. Harold is everything that James is not, handsome, charming, rich, and successful.

"Hello James, my name is Harold Atkins and I have a reservation for two." Harold responds with a smug pearly white smile. He releases his lines so well, that he could've easily been an A list actor, effortlessly going toe to toe with the likes of Brad Pit, Tom Cruise, and Denzel Washington. He is as slick as snot! James opens the reservation book and pretends to thumb through it.

"Alright Mr. Atkins, I see your name. If you would be so kind as to follow me, I will show you and your guest to your seats." James retorts as he flashes a fake smile. He knows exactly where to have them seated. Harold always calls thirty to forty-five minutes before hand to make sure his same section will be ready for him. He always sits in the private area divided from the rest of the restaurant, and devoid of windows. This is how he has kept the same game working since forever. Harold and Amanda take their seats. The passion between them is as hot as ever. Amanda knows that what they're doing is wrong, but she feels so alive when she is in his presence. He makes her feel something that she hasn't felt in years. Something that Carl has failed to produce.

"So what made you want me back? I thought you were trying to work it out with your husband?" Harold asks as he studies Amanda. She is even more beautiful than he remembers. He knows that he's dead wrong. He knows the consequences of messing with a married woman. He remembers what happened with their last go round, all of the drama and unneeded stress; but something about it, is like a drug. It gives him a rush unlike any other thing that he has experienced. The thrill of messing with a married woman is unrivaled. It is a burning desire, one that can only be satisfied with the right element.

"I couldn't stay away...I tried to make it work, but...we're just too far gone. It's dead. Our relationship is over. Carl still wants to hang on, but it's useless. He's stuck on weed again and chain smoking those disgusting cigarettes! Plus, he's still out of work and on unemployment." Amanda feels terrible, speaking so unfavorably about her husband, but she has to vent to someone. It's just too much to keep bottled in, she's tried to tell her friends Trisha and Alicia, but they have already told her that she was stupid for going back in the first place! The only thing that they are useful for is providing a good alibi. "Harold I'm ready for you...I'm ready for us." Amanda places her hand on Harold's hand. They look into each other's eyes, and share a deep intimate moment of reflection. Harold really enjoys her company. His feelings for Amanda are deeper than any that he's had for any other woman. If it weren't for the fact of the both of them being married to other people, he would have already devoted his all to her without second thought. His success is what keeps him trapped in his marriage, all of the money that he stands to lose in divorce, hangs over his head like a cloud full of rain. Getting a divorce would be a sticky, costly situation, one that would surely drain at least half of his assets and net worth. The saying, "It's cheaper to keep her", has never rung so true.

Within minutes of their conversation, a waiter arrives to take their order. Harold, such a creature of habit, orders one of his usual dishes, and Amanda orders a fresh salad. With everything that she's going through, she doesn't have the appetite to stomach a full lunch.

1:04pm: The happy couple leaves the restaurant hand in hand with bright smiles on their faces. Malcolm snaps more pictures as they enter the vehicle. The car slowly pulls off. Malcolm starts up his vehicle and follows cautiously behind them, maintaining a three-car distance at all times.

1:18pm: The couple arrives back at Harold's company. After a few moments of kissing and fondling, Harold exits the vehicle and goes back to work. From the time they parked, up to the time Harold went back into work, Malcolm has been filming. Harold's days of being a two timing cheat are numbered, and he is completely oblivious to it.

2:30pm: Harold receives a call from an unknown woman.

"Hi baby, whatcha doing?" A sweet sultry voice inquires on the other end of the line.

"Nothing, just thinking about you my love" is Harold's response.

"Real smooth Mr. Charm the girls' panties off." She responds "You know I've been missing you sexy. I need to see you." She gushes as Harold smiles in approval of what he's hearing. He loves when he gets them to that point. It's only been a couple of days, and she's already having withdrawal.

"So what kind of panties do you have on?" Harold boldly inquires as he leans back in his plush leather, ultra comfortable office chair.

"I have on the kind that was made for you to take off." She responds in an equally bold manner.

"That's what I like to hear, so are we still on for tomorrow."

"Hell yeah baby, ain't nothing stopping that!" A knock on Harold's office door, interrupts his phone conversation

"Come in" he says aloud. "Hey baby, let me call you back a little later. I've got some business to handle."

"Okay don't forget"

"I won't, I promise." Harold hangs up the phone just as his voluptuous secretary enters the room. Despite her cute face, tantalizing curvaceous frame, and soft smooth medium brown skin, she is probably one of the only women in his life that he has not slept with. The sole reason for this is that he refuses to mix business with pleasure.

"Hello Mr. Atkins, an urgent package just arrived for you," the secretary says as she places a medium sized envelope on his desk.

"Okay. Thanks Michelle." He responds before picking it up. After Michelle leaves, he opens the envelope. He pulls out a handwritten letter. As he reads the letter, the look on his face sours. The lipstick imprint at the bottom of the letter only makes it worse. In a fit of anger, Harold rips and crumbles the letter.

4:02pm: Harold makes a call to his wife. While the phone is ringing, he is entertaining lustful thoughts of Amanda. His thoughts abruptly come to a screeching halt, at the sound of his daughter's sweet innocent voice.

"Hello?"

"Hey Janice honey, its dad, let me speak to your mom." He states in the same soft voice he always uses when talking to his precious angel.

"Okay Dad. I love you, hold on," Janice says before putting down the phone. He can hear her calling for Denise as he waits patiently on the phone. Her footfalls echo loudly as she runs to get her mom. Thoughts of Amanda still stalk his conscious. The way her soft skin feels when pressed against his, the taste of her hard erect nipples, the sound of her climax; he almost gets erect just thinking about it.

"Hello" Denise's voice draws his attention back to the phone.

"Hey honey, I was just calling to say I miss you, and I will probably be in late. The…" Before Harold can finish his statement, Denise interjects.

"Are you serious? What is it this time, work, your buddies, or is it something else? I'm really getting sick of this! You would think that a person of your stature, a successful business owner, would have time for his family!"

"Hold on baby, you really need to take it down a notch. I told you that with the company expansions coming into play that I was going to be putting more hours in at the office. Besides, I don't even go out with my buddies that often. On average, I go out with them like what, once every two to three weeks?" Harold clearly presents his case while managing to keep a cool head and maintain a pleasant tone. He has done this so many times that, he has mastered the art of diffusing a potentially dramatic situation.

"Well..."

"Exactly, so let's not cause any discord in our relationship. I love you and I think about you all the time. Everything that I'm doing is for us, but anyway, I set up something special for Saturday. So when you talk to Britney, make sure to tell her that she's on sitter duty for that evening. It will be just us, no Janice, no Britney, no work, and none of my Buddies, just us." Harold knows that mentioning a date for Saturday, is all that he needs to do to appease her. He's mastered the art of managing her emotions.

"Umm, okay" Is the only thing that Denise can manage to utter. She wants to be angry with him; she wants to continue giving him a piece of her mind, but a great stillness from within starts to manifest. "I love you too Harold," she cannot believe herself. She is ashamed of the way that she lets him gain control over her. She feels weak, and in some weird way dependant on his influence over her life. She starts to doubt her gut feelings of Harold's infidelity. She desperately wants to believe in his innocence. She wants to believe his explanations and lies. She wants to believe him, but at the same time, she feels like it would be foolish to do so. She contemplates whether she should proceed with the attorney. "What if I'm being paranoid?" She thinks to herself as she glances over at her precious angel coloring with her custom art set. The art set is rather expensive for a five year old, but Harold only wants the best for the ladies in his life. He has done very well by them. He has provided them with a life that most, only dream of living.

"Oh yeah, and tell Britney that I'll be able to pick her up from Stacy's house around eight okay? Oh and one more thing, remember that lingerie set that I bought you for Valentine's Day?"

"Yes, the black and silver bustier."

"Yup, that's the one. How about you wear that for me tonight, I feel like doing something special!" Harold says in an exquisitely smooth voice, a voice that makes Denise melt every time she hears it. She feels so foolish, but at the same time, she feels so in love. "Honey doll, are you still there?"

"Yes baby, I was just reminiscing about last Valentine's Day." She murmurs as she tries to shake her feelings of doubt.

"Good. Well I'm about to get back to work. I will call you when I'm on my way home."

"Okay," she hangs up the phone and reflects more on her situation.

5:04pm: Harold leaves and goes to the car garage. He checks over his shoulder before getting into one of his favorite cars, a cranberry colored BMW 5 series. Once inside, he sprays himself with his own self-mixed cologne. It is a combination of pricy oils and wintergreen alcohol. He uses it, because he hates to smell like another man. He loves individuality. It is something that he swears by.

5:17pm: Harold stops at a Wal-Mart Supercenter. Malcolm inconspicuously parks and waits a few seconds before following him in. Within minutes of being in the store, Malcolm catches Harold flirting with a woman in produce. After a few minutes of conversation, they exchange numbers.

5:26pm: Harold leaves the store with several incriminating items, condoms, a can of whipped cream, and rose petals, as well as a "One Direction" DVD/CD combo pack. Malcolm manages to get everything on film. He is such a pro at what he does. He gets such a rush from doing things right. As Harold is walking to his car, he notices Malcolm. He pauses for a moment as he stares at the man. Malcolm tenses up slightly, but is able to maintain his composure. He slightly looks away and acts as if he is checking a text message on his phone. Harold stops glancing and resumes his walk back to his car.

5:48pm: Harold arrives at a moderately classy hotel on the outskirts of town. Malcolm, always three cars length behind, pulls into the parking lot subsequently thereafter. Harold gets out of his car and dials up a number on his cell phone. His smooth walk is uninterrupted by his interaction with the phone.

"I'm here," he says in a crisp, effectively smooth voice, as he walks through the automatic double doors of the hotel. Once inside, Harold goes to the front desk and starts talking to the attendant. With courteous smiles exchanged, the attendant hands him a keycard. Harold walks from the desk, and continues towards the elevators.

Harold arrives at his destination. He steps out of the elevator on the fifth floor and walks a little ways down the hall before stopping in front of one of the doors. He gently swipes the key card through the slot, and the green light flashes, accompanied by a soft beep. Upon entering the room, the atmosphere arouses his senses; lit candles catches his eyes, soft music playing in the background captivates his ears, and a sweet womanly fragrance seeps into his nostrils. He hears soft splashing coming from the bathroom. Based on the sounds, he assumes that his fantasy is getting ready for a session of ecstasy. He sets down his things, and grabs the rose pedals out of the bag. He scatters a few over the bed and proceeds to the bathroom. He gently opens the door and his eyes immediately take in the full naked beauty of Amanda. She smiles affectionately at Harold as she gracefully rinses off the bubbles from her bath. Like performing a scene from a movie, Harold begins placing rose petals on the floor before his naked glistening Puerto Rican beauty. He magically creates a path leading from the tub, and ending at the bed. Amanda's eyes light up at the sight of the path. She has a notion to come out of the bathroom naked, but decides to stick with her game plan. She dries herself off and grabs the Victoria's Secret bag from off of the bathroom counter. She pulls out the contents of the bag and giddily puts them on.

Harold is getting himself ready for the moment as well. He has been anxious to get another crack at Amanda since the night after the club when she was out with her friends. Amanda emerges from the bathroom in a sheer black mesh and shimmering silver eyelet bustier. Harold's excitement level instantly rises at the sight of her scantily clad curvaceous figure.

"Come and get it Daddy!" She seductively says as she gives Harold her best cum hither look. He mentally salivates at the thought of satisfying his sexual appetite. Harold obeys like a good soldier. Their lips meet in an explosion of passion. They are unable to contain their burning desire. Amanda hops onto Harold and he carries her to the rose pedal covered bed. He places her down and begins attacking her body with a barrage of soft wet kisses. He carefully removes the bustier with a surgeon's precision. Amanda moans in anticipation. She can hardly wait to feel him back inside of her. Each kiss brings her closer to the point no return, she can no longer wait; she wants his hard strong manhood inside of her. Harold pauses the foreplay session and grabs the whipped cream and condoms. He smiles at Amanda's exposed flesh as he shakes the can of cream. He breaks off the cap, and sprays circles of cream around her nipples, and a zigzagging trail from her breasts to her sweet wet spot. Harold slowly starts slurping and kissing off the white sugary goodness from Amanda's soft supple, golden skin. She moans with each soft kiss applied to her freshly bathed skin. The kisses send electric jolts throughout her body. He continues sopping whipped cream from off of his Puerto Rican fantasy as he removes the rest of his attire. Within seconds, he is completely disrobed and ready to give her what she has been anticipating. He finishes with the cream and then submerges his mouth into her wet throbbing love patch. Amanda's moans get louder and she begins to squirm. His tongue motions clear all other thoughts out of her mind. The head is so good, that it is all she can focus on. It has completely consumed her mind. She grabs at Harold's hair as he passionately French kisses her throbbing juicy pussy.

"Oh shit baby I'm ready!"She exclaims in a heavy, breathy tone.

"You're not ready till I say you're ready." Harold responds in an authoritative manner. He loves to be in control. He continues as she releases his hair and alternates to gripping the hotel bedding. Amanda is on the verge of an explosion, when Harold stops. Her build up abruptly comes to a halt.

"Fuck!" She exhales as she regains control over herself. Harold brings himself up from Amanda's moist fertile playground. He slips on a condom and penetrates her honey pot. She quivers as he enters. Erotic energy crashes onto Amanda as Harold dives deeper into her love/lust pit. Their movements are slow and synchronized. They move to the rhythm of unadulterated lust. She shakes with every stroke of penetration. Sweat trickles down his forehead and back, as he vigorously moves between her thighs. He dominates her with his technique. Every single movement sends a surge of electricity through her vessel.

She erupts in a fit of orgasmic pleasure. She clings to the sheets for dear life as her body shakes and shutters from the impact of satisfaction. The minutes fly by as he drills between her walls. Tears fall from her face, as she takes in short shallow breaths. Then in a climatic instance, he releases his penned up tension.

Harold and Amanda lie in the aftermath of passion. Amanda's head swirls with euphoric emotions. She knows that what she is feeling is real. She does not care about the consequences of her acts. She is ready to leave Carl; she is done with being an unhappily married woman.

"I love you baby!" She blurts out, clearly not thinking about the ramifications of such a statement. Harold, caught off guard by Amanda's confession of love does not know how to respond. Even though he feels something similar, he is not sure if he should say it back. In spite of their troublesome situation, He honestly feels true love for the very first time.

"I love you too Amanda." He utters as he finally acknowledges his feelings. After letting her know they have mutual feelings, he gets up and goes to the shower. She follows him. They spend a few more loving moments in the shower before they wash up, get dressed, and go back to their less than satisfactory lives.

7:31pm: Harold and Amanda leave the hotel. He walks her to her car, and they kiss and embrace before he walks back to his vehicle and leaves.

8:02pm: Harold arrives at Stacy's house. He calls Britney's cell phone.

"Hey Honey bear, I'm here." He says as she answers.

"Okay Papa bear, I'll be out shortly." His daughter responds. He looks at himself in the mirror. He feels bad but good at the same time. He secretly hopes that neither one of his daughters will end up with a man like himself. He would die if they ever found out about his double life. He loves them too much to hurt them. He tries to rationalize his behavior as he sits alone in his idling BMW. A few minutes later, his daughter Britney comes out. He straightens himself up before she enters the car.

"Hey honey, how was your day?" Harold asks as he studies his daughter. She favors her mother so much. Her bright green eyes and light brown hair, instantly invokes the thought in Harold's mind. He cannot help but to think about Denise. He maintains a smile to hide the guilt that he is feeling.

"My day was pretty awesome; me and Stacy finished the group project. We are going to totally ace it!" Britney responds excitedly. He's so proud of her. She's growing up so fast, he shutters at the thought of her dating. He knows that he only has a couple more years until doomsday, the day Denise and himself agreed to let her begin dating. He pushes those thoughts aside and remembers the gift he purchased for her. He reaches under his seat, and pulls out the "One Direction" combo pack.

"Here you go honey." He says with a smile on his face as he hands her the gift.

"Oh wow you remembered! Thanks Dad!" She exclaims before giving him a big hug.

"You're welcome honey. You've earned it. I'm proud of you. You're doing so well in school; it's the least I could do. It's just my way of saying keep up the good work Honey bear."

"I will dad, I promise" Britney blurts as she gushes with joy. He put the car in reverse and they start their trip home.

8:20pm: Harold and Britney arrive home. As they enter the house, Harold remembers the letter he received earlier. The thought of it makes him cringe. He knows that he has to get out of the marriage before Denise finds out about everything. As Harold steps into the front room, Janice runs to him and wraps her little arms around his much larger frame. "Daddy," she blurts as she continues to embrace her hero. Harold picks up his precocious little angel.

"Hi Honey bunny, Daddy missed you!" He states as he holds her in his arms. "So what did you do today?" He asks as he places her back down and stares into her big gray eyes, her long brown hair, neatly bunched into a ponytail.

"I went to school and I came home, and colored. I made you a picture too Papa Bear!" She says in her cute small voice.

"Oh wow really, I would love to see it." He responds before she runs out of the room. She returns seconds later with a crude homemade picture. The picture is of a stickman with a tie and scribbled black hair. The stickman is sitting in an office with a big window, and a large yellow colored sun with a smiley face drawn on it. "This is a nice picture, do you mind if I take this to work and hang it up in my office?" Harold asks as he stares at the artwork.

"Sure Dad, of course you can. I made it for you!"

"Okay now how about you get ready for bed. And once you're ready, I will come and read you a bedtime story."

"Alright Papa Bear," She responds before ripping out of the room.

After their children are asleep, Harold and Denise engage in an act of lustful sex. The bustier helps Harold stay focused on his fantasy, on his thoughts of Amanda. In the back of her head, Denise knows that she should have insisted that Harold wear a condom. She knows that he has been unfaithful, but she just can't will herself to do such a thing. His raw strokes feel so good, that part of her deems it a justifiable risk. After a lengthy emotional and mental debate, she gives in and lets lust take control. She gives in to the warmth of his body, the smell of his masculinity, the rhythm of his labor. In an instant, his raw love makes her succumb, to the euphoric ecstasy, that only it can induce. Tears fall from her eyes as Harold continues thrusting himself inside of her warm wet walls. Deep down she wants to believe him, or rather, she wants to believe in him. She wants to have faith in what he claims, but regardless of how she feels, she knows it is over, and the moment that they are sharing, is only a temporary fix. It is merely an illusion of their former relationship that has long since died. Her biggest hindrances in breaking away from him are, the children, the love she has for him, and his irresistible sexual charm. He has her under control. He has her mind, body, and emotions under his thumb.

DAY 2

8:02am: Harold leaves his house adorned in golfing attire. He leaves his Cranberry BMW, and opts to take his silver S-class Mercedes Benz instead. Malcolm is parked a few houses up the street. He watches as Harold gets in the silver Benz, and pulls out of the driveway. Malcolm revs up his car and follows him. He is determined to get enough evidence by week's end.

8:21am: Harold arrives at Grover Lane Apartments. A female comes out of the apartment. Her dark brown skin, leggy frame, and fashionista flair, instantly arouses Malcolm's curiosity. Even in golfer wear, she is still a stunning sight. Her makeup and hair are flawless, and her smile looks like it can capture rays of sunlight. Harold, always the perfect gentleman, gets out and opens the passenger door for her. They share a quick passionate kiss before she gets in his vehicle. As they leave the apartment complex, Malcolm follows not far behind. Harold's female companion is Vicki Phillips. Harold is fifteen years her senior. He knows that their relationship is a temporary fling, so he does not have any feelings invested into it. At this point in his life, he only has feelings for one woman, and it's not Denise. He contemplates dropping Vicki back off and contacting Amanda. His heart yearns for her. He finally understands what it means to be in love. The fact that she is still with Carl, puts a halt on his plans of being exclusive. He decides to stop thinking about his love, and focuses on the day at hand.

8:43am: Harold and Vicki, arrive at "Solon Golf ways" golf course in Tree Bridge Hts. For the next forty-five minutes or so, the two lust birds, kiss, flirt, and half-ass their way through the course. Malcolm captures every single inappropriate kiss, touch, and grope. Harold's prowess to juggle the opposite sex amazes Malcolm.

9:31am: Harold and Vicki leave the golf course. Vicki can barely keep her hands off Harold. She starts by softly massaging his thigh, and ends up giving him a hand job. For the most part, Harold maintains control of the vehicle, only swerving a few times during the trip. Malcolm takes notice of the swerving and can only imagine what is occurring in the car. Vicki continues stoking Harold's stiff hard manhood. Harold enjoys every stroke of her hand.

"If you make it come up, you're going to have to clean it up." He warns as he continues to maintain his composure, and keep the vehicle cruising at a moderately steady speed.

"I always clean up when I'm done playing" She wittily shoots back.

"Touché, that's a good girl." Harold murmurs as he flashes a lustful smile at Vicki. He feels his climax level rising as she increases the passion of her strokes. "Oh yeah baby, I'm about to cum!" He blurts out in a quick breathy tone. Vicki responds by quickly pulling a hanker chief out of her purse and catching Harold's oozing load.

"Ahh" Harold moans as the car swerves slightly from his brief loss of control. "Whew fuck!" He exclaims as a big smile forms on his face. Vicki finishes the clean up, and places Harold partially limp penis back into his pants.

9:52am: Harold and Vicki make a stop at a coffee shop on Grand street called "Palace of Beans". Malcolm manages to find a parking spot with a suitable view of the shop. He films as much as possible. Harold is oblivious to Malcolm. He is so engrossed in Vicki, that he barely pays attention to anything else.

"So what do you want to do after we leave from here?" Vicki asks as she drinks her Café Mocha.

"It's up to you baby, it's your special day. We can do whatever; it's all about pleasing you." Harold responds as he carefully sips his French Vanilla

"Well how about we go back to my place, and you show me just how much you're willing to please me." Vicki says as she flashes a quick lust infused smile.

"Okay, I'm all for it. It's only fair that you get yours too!" Harold murmurs in between sips of his steamy hot beverage.

"That's what I like about baby; you really know how to treat a girl!" Vicki responds, totally smitten by his pleasing personality.

10:13am: Harold and Vicki leave the coffee shop. Malcolm gets more footage of the happy lustful couple. Still amazed by the dark brown beauty, Malcolm finds himself entertaining thoughts of sampling her brown sugar. He feels himself starting to dislike Harold even more. He can hardly wait for the prick to get what he deserves. Harold and the luscious Vicki, get back in the Silver Benz, and head off.

10:41am: They arrive back at the apartment complex. Harold swiftly parks his car. He and Vicki head towards the apartment with a lustful since of urgency. Once inside the apartment, Harold grabs Vicki, and hoists her onto his waist. They kiss and fondle as they make their way up the stairs. Primal instinct has taken control; they are lost in the wiles of lust. The fires of their passion roar as they reach the top of the stairs. Vicki fumbles around in her purse for the keys, while she and Harold continue getting hot and heavy.

She finally manages to find them tucked underneath her makeup bag and various scraps of paper. They clumsily make their way to the door of her apartment suite, and after a few distracted attempts, she successfully unlocks it.

Once inside, they rip off each other's clothing in a fit of pure uninhibited lust. Their lust quickly escalates into a burning, all consuming wild fire. Harold carries his chocolate treat into the bedroom. In the bedroom, Vicki gets on her knees and takes Harold's manhood into her warm salivating mouth. She forms a tight smooth grip around his penis, with her soft full lips. The moistness of her mouth makes Harold's knees slightly buckle. She bobs her head back and forth on his impressively sized unit. She takes it in deep and feels her involuntary gag reflex kicking in. After a few moments of enjoyment, Harold picks Vicki up and forces her onto the bed. "I told you that it was about me pleasing you," he utters in a smooth bass tinged voice, before pouncing like a tiger catching its prey. He spreads and lifts her long brown legs apart, and begins his oral assault on her secret garden. His tongue passionately strokes her clitoris, alternating between circular and vertical motions. When her flowers are ready to bloom, he stops and instructs her to bend over the bed. Her top half rests on the bed, while he props her bottom half into the desired position. His forcefulness further stimulates her already engaged sex drive. Harold quickly slides on a condom, and thrusts his hard pulsating cock, balls deep into Vicki's chocolate, juicy snatch.

"Oh fuck!" She yells out in profane approval. Harold thrusts away inside of her tight wet box. She digs her nails into her silk sheets, and squirts her love as he continues drilling for pleasure. Her legs shake as her liquid lust runs down them. Harold is satisfying her just right. Vicki moans louder and louder as she sinks deeper and deeper into the pit of pleasure. Harold works her body like a double shift in a steel mill, hard and diligent. He is determined to leave his mark in her memory. He wants to make certain that she will reminisce about him for the rest of her natural life. Suddenly, like an act of a higher power, she dies sexually in an orgasmic fit. Her whole body shakes and tremors as he continues to stroke in her afterlife. He thrusts like a mighty thunder God. Vicki is completely out of it. From this day forward, until another champion lover replaces him, Harold is the best that she has ever had. He finishes and lets out a loud manly grunt. He gets his bearings, and exits her play land.

After taking a shower and getting dressed, Harold kisses Vicki, (who is now fast asleep), and leaves her apartment.

12:05pm: Harold leaves the apartment building. Malcolm, being ever so diligent, films every second of every step that Harold makes toward his car. Harold gets in his car and starts it up. Before he leaves the parking lot, his phone begins to ring. He looks at the phone's screen and sees Amanda's number. He quickly answers.

"Hello"

"Hi sexy, I wanna see you right now." Amanda says in a seductive voice.

"That sounds great baby, but now isn't a good time. I'm in the middle of something. How about I call you back once I get free?" Harold says as a means of stalling. He already knows what she wants, what she longs for. She longs to get fucked, long, and hard.

"Okay well don't keep me waiting too long, I need you Daddy." She states in a brazen sexual manner.

"Alright so what did you have in mind?" He inquires, even though knows what she wants. It is at this moment, that he comes to the realization that he can't do it anymore. He can't continue juggling multiple women. It has to end. Time is no longer on his side. The grays of wisdom are starting to creep in, and Karma is not far behind.

"I'm going to be at the Super 8 motel on Aurora Boulevard, room six. Don't keep me waiting too long." Amanda says with eagerness present in her voice.

"I won't, I promise." Harold responds as he turns the corner, and hits a main intersection. "Give me like forty minutes, I'll be there."

12:35pm: Harold pulls into the parking lot of the Super 8 motel, with his tail not far behind. Malcolm is astonished by the fact that Harold just left Vicki's apartment, and is now about to meet someone else at a motel.

"Talk about sexual addiction!" Malcolm mumbles as he gets his camera ready. "He's definitely here to see another chick. This guy is fucking disgrace!" He says aloud as he watches the latest part of Harold's extramarital saga. Harold parks his car and calls Amanda.

"I'm here." Harold utters into the phone as he heads to room six. Amanda opens the door just as Harold reaches it. Malcolm zooms in on them before Harold enters the room. He gets an excellent shot of them kissing before Harold goes in.

"It's about time you got here Papi; I was starting to get lonely." Amanda says as she rubs Harold's chest.

"Why so impatient senorita, good things come to those who wait." Harold responds as he lustfully scopes Amanda's lovely physique, in her tight revealing dark red mini dress.

"Well I've been waiting, so now I want that good thing!" Amanda says before planting her lips on Harold's and forcing her tongue inside of his mouth. Harold responds with mutual vigor. He forces Amanda up against the wall closest to the door. His hands fondle her luscious frame. They glide from her shapely legs, to underneath her dress. His fingers make contact with her bare, uncovered moist snatch.

"Surprise no panties." She says in an ultra seductive voice. He smiles in response and quickly undoes his pants. He throws caution to the wind, spreads her legs, and shoves his erect cock into her moist chocha.

"I Papi" Amanda exclaims as the hard warm penis thrusts into her sugar walls. Harold grabs both of her legs, hoists her up on his waist, and commences to fuck her roughly against the drab wallpaper covered wall. Lacking a condom, her wetness is much more intense than before. He feels her bare insides; every stroke draws him deeper into the act of copulation. He tries his best to convey his deep longing affection for her. In one swift motion, he lifts her from off of the wall and walks her over to the bed; all the while, still pumping away. His sexual prowess is indeed above average. He rests her on the edge of the bed, and props her legs on his shoulders. He continues hammering away in passionate rhythmic motions. She moans louder and louder, as her champion lover controls the situation.

"Oh fuck! I-I love you!" Amanda shouts as Harold fucks her sweet tight twat like a wild man.

"Yeah baby cum for Daddy!" He commands as he has his way with her.

"Oh Papi, I'm almost there! Ahh" Amanda yells as her legs twitch against Harold. His now sweat soaked shirt, sticks to his defined chest, as he wails away at his object of desire. "Here it comes! Oh!" Amanda moans before her volcano erupts. Her body vibrates as an instant effect of climatic pleasure. Harold feels himself nearing completion, and quickly slips out. He explodes over the outside of her fun zone.

"Better out than in...fuck!" he mumbles as he continues his release. He looks down at Amanda and sees Vicki! He shakes his head in disbelief. He looks back again, and sees Denise! He quickly closes his eyes. Amanda notices his weird behavior and addresses it.

"Are you okay?" She inquires as she reaches for something to catch Harold's now dripping load. Harold looks back at her and sees, just Amanda.

"Yeah...I'm okay. I just got little dizzy." He utters as he realizes the effect that his behavior is having on his psyche. He is lost in the sinful debacle that has become his life. His haphazard lifestyle has become an all-consuming addiction. He is blatantly in denial. He still thinks that he is in control, but in reality, he is completely lost. His lack of self-control is now comparable to that of a person addicted heavily to a vice. The kind that believes that they can quit anytime they desire to do so. His nose is wide open. He is desperately in need of an intervention. Amanda takes a moment for herself, while Harold rushes into the shower. She thinks about what has just occurred. She knows what she has to do, she has to end it today; she has to leave Carl! Amanda hears the water from the shower start up as she lies across the bed. She contemplates staying for the night and dealing with Carl tomorrow. She can no longer deal with the arguing and fighting. She is tired of using lies and excuses to hold on to an already failed marriage. She no longer wants to be the villainess. Carl has every right to act the way he acts. He is the victim. He is the one left with the trick, while she gets the treat. Amanda builds up her courage, and grabs her phone from off of the nightstand. Her anxiety level rises with each digit dialed. She feels a knot form in her stomach as she waits for Carl to answer.

"Amanda?" Carl says as he answers the phone. His mind is hazy, courtesy of marijuana.

"Yeah, it's me...umm I have to tell you something." She has been planning this day for weeks. She even made sure to take a week's worth of clothing and personal items. She waited until Carl fell asleep before hastily gathering her things, and slipping out. Carl waits in silence on the other end of the line, while Amanda struggles to finish her statement. His mind is already thinking the worst, and the paranoia induced by the weed, only amplifies his already dreadful thoughts.

"What, are we done?" He inquires, breaking the silence and helping the process along.

"Yeah, well…I…I can't do this anymore. I'm sick of arguing, I'm sick of the weed, the cigarettes, and your lack of motivation. You say you want to make things better, but your lack of action tells me something different. I'm not coming home tonight, we're through…" Amanda's words trail off, and the silence sets back in. Carl, still in a catatonic stupor, is slow to react. He was already somewhat expecting to hear it. It's been a long time coming.

"What…why? I mean…why can't we work it out? I love you," Is all that he can force himself to say. He wonders, if that is in fact her true reason, or if she is being unfaithful.

"Look, it's done. I'm done! You're hindering me, bringing me down…"

"Who is he?" Carl blurts out, cutting Amanda off like a car in traffic.

"What are you talking about? Didn't you hear everything I just said?" She questions as she contemplates revealing the truth.

"I heard what you just said, but did you hear what I just asked you? WHO IS HE?" His voice elevates with a harsh undertone.

"It doesn't matter, what matters is the fact that I'm done!" Amanda hears Harold shutting off the water. "I gotta go, don't try to find me...I'll be back for my things by the end of the week." She says before abruptly ending the conversation. At that moment, Harold emerges from the bathroom with nothing but a towel on. His glistening ripped body excites Amanda. She pictures herself waking up to him, morning after morning for the rest of her natural life. She's in love, and is ready to take it to the next level. "I broke it off with Carl." She blurts out as she continues to stare at her champion stallion.

"You did what?" Harold responds, completely thrown off by the revelation.

"I...I ended it. I'm done. I only want to be with you. I really want to give us a chance." She confesses, putting it all on the line, placing all or nothing on her sure fire bet.

"Whoa you did what? I..." He pauses as he searches for the right way to convey his thoughts. Unlike Amanda, He knows that his breaks will not be as clean, especially with Denise and his children. Vicki is just a fling of the moment, so he is not too concerned with her; his only concern is his family and wealth. "Baby slow down, I feel the same as you, and I'm ready to have a fresh start too, but if I leave my wife, I stand to lose at least half of everything I've worked for. That's half of the fruits of my labor, half of my blood, sweat, and tears. Now is not the time..." Amanda feels anger starting to rise from within.

"So what are you saying? Are you trying to say that you're not willing to walk away and have a clean slate because money is involved? I don't know about you, but I'm tired of sneaking around and keeping secrets. I'm ready to commit to you and only you! Harold...I...I love you." Amanda says as she feels her eyes get warm with emotion. She doesn't want Harold to see her cry, but she can't help it. She's in love and ready to devote her all to him.

"Hold on honey, I didn't mean it like that...I love you too, it's just that...well the money doesn't mean as much as the impression that it will leave on my daughters. I want to have a fresh start...I want to be able to just run off with you and start anew. I really do, but in all honesty...I need a little bit of time." Harold says as he watches the first few tears run down Amanda's rosy red cheeks. He rushes over to comfort her, and they spend a few moments in silence. Harold holds her tight as he starts to feel tears forming in his eyes. Time stops, as they sit alone in room six of the budget motel, crying, comforting one another, and both wishing that things were not so complicated. After some time has lapsed, Harold breaks the silence. "Just give me a week." He murmurs, not particularly sure of what he's committing to. He is formulating off the cuff. "I'm leaving Denise in a week." He states flatly, devoid of any emotion. He knows what he has to do. The gears are in motion. There is no turning back. He does not want to lose the best thing that has ever happened to him. He does not want to lose Amanda!

"Are you sure about that?" Amanda questions, as she looks Harold into the eyes.

"Yes, I'm positive. I'm ready to be happy." He says with a smile. Amanda and Harold share one last passionate kiss before he gets dressed.

1:45pm: Harold leaves room six. Malcolm, on the verge of

falling asleep barely notices him. He only manages to get a couple of shots of Harold walking back to his car. Thoughts cloud Harold's mind as he gets into his vehicle. He is a troubled man. His heart is heavy and his conscience is eating him alive. He contemplates if true love is worth losing millions. Even if the courts did award Denise with half of his wealth, he would still have enough to maintain a comfortable lifestyle, and his business would supply him with a nice stream of future earnings. He is so absorbed in his thoughts that he again fails to notice Malcolm. He starts up his luxury car, and heads home.

2:31pm: Harold arrives back home. He tries his best to block out everything. He goes in the house, and puts on the facade of a happy loving husband. He sees Denise in the kitchen, and heads straight towards her. She is in the middle of juicing some new concoction that she more than likely, got off some daytime talk show or weblog. She was once a shopaholic, but that got old after a couple of years. So now, she's more of a homebody. TV and the internet, has become her life. She has so many shows recorded on her DVR; it is a wonder that she finds time to watch them all. Judge Judy, America's Next Top Model, and The Wendy Williams Show, are just some of the shows frequently captured on it. Harold slowly creeps up behind her and grabs her around the waist. She involuntarily jumps and lets out a short shriek.

"Harold!" She snaps as she turns around to see the man that was once the love of her life, but is now the cause of her heartache.

"Hey baby, I missed you," he responds before kissing her.

"You missed me? I'm surprised, considering how busy you've been lately." She retorts, clearly expressing her disdain for his frequent absence and negligence.

"Yes, I missed you silly! I've been thinking...how about we have a nice family night out, just you, the girls, and me. We could go catch a movie, and maybe have a bite to eat afterwards." His family night request, really throws her for a loop. She wonders if maybe he's feeling guilty, or if he genuinely wants to make up for lost time. It's hard to tell with a man like Harold. Denise has never found any telltale marks or evidence to substantiate her suspicions of infidelity; no scratches, hickies, or unaccounted for periods of time, no clothing, makeup, or other personal items from other females, left in any of his cars. She has even gone as far as checking his phone every night for an entire month! Unbeknownst to Denise, Harold keeps a second prepaid phone stashed away, and goes to great lengths to keep his vehicles and body evidence free. Harold has been unfaithful, almost as long as they have been married! He knows all of the ins and outs. He has mastered the art of deception. Hiding his sexual dalliances from Denise has become second nature. Most of them have never lasted longer than three months. Harold gets bored easily with the majority of the ones he attracts. Quite a few of them, like Vicki, are young, naïve, and easily blinded by money. Amanda is something different; she has something that captures his full attention. There is a factor she possesses, which makes it close to impossible for him to let her go. Even when Carl found out about their affair the first time around, they still managed to keep a slight connection. It took a lot of money and a fall guy, to keep Denise from getting wind of it. Even after all of that, he still chooses to carry on with it. Their relationship breaks almost every rule in his book and goes drastically against his better judgment. "So what do you say? Are you up for it?" He questions while forcing a slightly exaggerated smile.

"Well, I guess. I mean it's not like we get a chance to do things together often." Denise agrees. She figures that it will be good for the kids to see them together, and for them all to have a good time. It has been ages since they have had a family outing.

3:32pm: Harold and his family leave the house. They hop into a black Cadillac Escalade, and pull out of the driveway. Malcolm figures that it would be a good time to catch a break. He starts up his car, and heads out to get a bite to eat.

DAY 3

"Hi honey, I'll be home in a bit. I'm just going out with the guys to a have a couple of beers okay?" Harold says on the phone to his wife as he pulls up to Grover Lane apartments. He has done this type of thing so many times, that it has become second nature. Part of him somewhere deep down knows it's wrong, but his very essence yearns for the thrill of being unfaithful and getting away with it. He steps out of his cranberry red BMW, and walks up to the apartment building. He has the confidence and prowess of a seasoned veteran. He is like an MVP athlete; he knows how to play the field like the back of his hand. He knows every lie, every alibi, what gifts will smooth things over when situations get hairy, and most importantly, he knows how to pull out and not get too involved! He thinks that he knows it all, but he is still unaware of

Malcolm. He watches as Harold's fingers gracefully glide over the security system's keypad. Malcolm records him effortlessly pick the four numbers to gain access to his jackpot. Within seconds, Vicki answers.

"Hello" she says in a sweet sensuous manner.

"Hey baby, it's me" Harold responds in a smooth cocky tone.

"Okay sexy I'm buzzing you in right now. I'll be on my way down in a minute." Vicki responds before a loud buzzer begins screaming. Harold pulls the door open, and casually strolls inside of the lobby area. Within a matter of minutes, he can see a pair of long luscious legs gracefully make their way down towards him. The rest of the package is equally as stunning. She is a sweet temptation that Harold is ready to indulge. "I'm really going to miss having fun with her." He thinks as he continues to stare at the gorgeous dark beauty. She greets him with a warm smile and an even warmer hug. He feels his manly senses awaken as he embraces her flawless frame.

"So you couldn't wait till seven huh?" She asks as she continues to smile at the handsomely devilish Harold.

"Well when you have gifts under the tree, you always want to wake up early to open them right?" He responds with flirtatious charm.

"Whoa tiger, save that for later," She responds while grabbing his hand. Malcolm bears witness yet again, to Harold exiting the building in the company of Vicki. He escorts her to his car, and opens the passenger door for her like a perfect gentleman.

6:54pm: The handsome couple arrives at Toni's. He lets Vicki out of the car, and hands off the keys to the valet. After passing off the keys, he opens the restaurant door, and escorts her inside. Once inside, he makes eye contact with James. James already knows the routine.

"Hello folks, welcome to Toni's. How may I help you?" He says as he puts on the whole routine, all the while, laughing in his head. He's done it so many times, and has seen so many different women with Harold, that he is amazed that he still manages to find new ones.

"Hello James my name is Harold, and I have a reservation for two." He says as flashes the same fake plastered on smile like many times before. James shows them to Harold's "special" booth, and returns back to the greeter podium. Harold contemplates whether he should break it off over diner, or keep it going and have one last moment of intimacy later at her apartment. Thoughts of Amanda's decision, replay in his head. The memory of them crying together in the budget motel room haunts him. Her leaving Carl has really complicated things. He feels guilty as he stares across the table at Vicki. He decides to appease both sides, and end his fling with Vicki after one last roll in the hay.

"Umm I had a great time yesterday. You're starting to be like a drug, I'm getting addicted to you." Vicki says as she stares into Harold's grayish blue eyes. Harold is lost in deep thought. Things are definitely starting to bother him. For the first time in years, his conscience is really getting the best of him. "Hello? Are you alright?" Vicki asks, snapping Harold out his trance-like state.

"Yeah, I'm good. I'm just a little tired from work." He responds as a waitress arrives to take their order.

"Hello, welcome to Toni's, my name is Jennifer, and I will be your waitress for this evening. What would you like to drink?" She asks as she hands them both menus. Jennifer tries to keep her focus on the both of them and not just Harold, but his strikingly handsome looks, make it a challenge to say the least. She manages to break his intoxicating spell, and shifts her focus to his flawless date. The dark dazzling beauty, with flawless black short cut hair, is a sharp contrast to her pale dull skin, bleached split ends, and chipped nail polish. She knows that the chances of a man like him noticing a girl like her are slimmer than an anorexic supermodel.

"Hello Jennifer. Well for starters, we would like a bottle of 1998 Veuve Clicquot La Grande Dame. We would also like an order of Shrimp Rillettes."

"Okay sir, I will be right back with your bottle and appetizers." Jennifer says before walking away. Vicki is impressed with his choices. She loves the way he takes control and handles things.

"So where do you see this going?" Vicki asks as she looks intensely at Harold. He hates when a woman asks that question. It usually means that she wants to be a bigger part of his life. It also means that she has some doubts about what he wants. Harold hates this part, and always tries to avoid it, because once they reach this point, they begin to attach and invest themselves emotionally. He seriously has second thoughts about one last sexual encounter.

"Well, it's still fairly early in our situation, and at the moment, I can't really say; I don't want to say something misleading, or make a commitment. I mean, we're still getting to know one another. I have a three month rule, and the rule is to wait until month three to decide whether to take it to the next level, or call it quits." Vicki is a little disappointed in his response, but she respects his honesty.

"Okay, I respect your honesty. I really do, but that's not what I wanted to hear. I mean, it's been magical between us and I'm really feeling what we have. The spontaneity, the excitement, and you have a sense of class about you that many of the men I've dealt with don't." Vicki places her hand on Harold's hand. "Look baby, all I'm saying is that, I don't want to let go of something so good. I don't want to let go of you!" Vicki's words hit Harold like a freight train.

"Damn it's too late! She's in too deep!" Harold thinks as he feels the warmth of Vicki's hand resting on top of his. He wants to pull out and cut the date short. He wants to call Amanda. He is ready to quit his games and come clean. Jennifer comes back with their bottle of wine and appetizers. She notices the mood at the table has changed.

"So, are you folks ready to order?" She inquires as she shifts her attention back to doing her job.

"Umm yes, give me the Steak and Shrimp Scampi Medley with steamed broccoli and white rice. Also, I want the steak medium rare and my lovely lady will have…"

"I will have a sautéed chicken breast, and a side of shrimp Scampi with rice pilaf." Vicki interjects.

"Okay I will be right back with your meals." Jennifer says before grabbing their menus and leaving.

"So are we cool?" Harold asks, sensing dissention between them. He opens up the bottle of wine, and fills both of their glasses.

"Yeah we're fine, just fine." Vicki says before gulping down a considerable portion of her wine. The tone of her voice has changed significantly. Harold understands that his response to her inquiry, has rubbed her the wrong way. He sips some of his wine as he thinks of what he really wants to do with her. He just wants to have a little bit more fun before he relinquishes his access to her. The rest of the dinner, goes off without a hitch, they enjoy their food, and keep the conversation to a minimum. The more Vicki drinks, the less upset she becomes.

"So are you ready for dessert?" Harold asks as he finishes his meal.

"No, not really, I just want to go back to my place and get fucked." Vicki says bluntly "So are we gonna fuck or what?" She questions. Her straight forwardness catches Harold completely off guard. It is exactly what he wants, sex and no feelings.

"Okay, as soon as I get the check we're out." He responds, blocking out thoughts of Amanda and replacing them with thoughts of fucking Vicki. He fantasizes about having Vicki's long legs wrapped around him as he pounds her sweet in between. Jennifer returns to the table.

"So would you care for any dessert?" She asks as she clears off the table.

"No, we're done. Can you bring us the check?" Harold responds as he anticipates getting in Vicki's panties for one last hurrah.

"Okay sir, I will be right back with it." Jennifer says before hurrying off.

After paying for the meals, and leaving Jennifer and James significant tips, Harold and Vicki leave Toni's. They are both feeling the effects of being slightly inebriated, Vicki more so.

7:47pm Harold and Vicki, are seen exiting the restaurant and waiting for the valet. Malcolm starts up his car, and continues recording. The valet attendant returns a few moments later with Harold's car. As usual, he lets Vicki in before himself. Once he is in, they speed off into the night, with Malcolm following behind like a shadow.

Inside the cranberry colored BMW, erotic music plays through the customized BOSE sound system. Vicki gets hornier by minute. She is hurt, the only thing she wants, is a good fuck, and some much needed rest. She wishes that she had her very own special someone to ease her lonely nights, but is willing to make due with a few moments of pleasure instead.

"Now when we get in, I want straight fucking, I don't want any kissing, soft touching, or cuddling. I just want you to fuck the shit outta me, and then be on your way." Vicki says in a slightly slurred manner. She feels no love. The hurt has brought on the lust bug big time. Harold does not respond. He just keeps his eyes focused on the road, and wonders if he heard her correctly. "Did you hear me? I want you to fuck the shit out of this black wet pussy! I want you to make me cum all over your hard white dick!" Vicki's aggressiveness is really starting to turn him on. He can hardly wait to oblige her demands.

"I heard you loud and clear. I'm going to fuck the shit out of that black pussy!" Harold proclaims with absolute confidence.

8:22pm: Harold's car pulls into Vicki's apartment complex. He parks and wastes no time getting Vicki out. Once inside her apartment, they get right down to business. Harold lifts Vicki, and carries her into the bedroom. He does not even waste time removing her panties, he moves them to the side, and lets his fingers warm her up. He fingers her aggressively. He rubs his thumb back and forth over Vicki's clitoris, while plunging his middle finger in and out of her sweet nectar pit. Vicki moans loudly in approval, as he continues to warm her up. Vicki writhes and shakes as Harold titillates her sweet spot. His efforts are fruitful; she pops into a climatic seizure and squirts all over the sheets.

"Oh fuck!" She exhales as she catches her breath. Her legs shake uncontrollably as Harold gets his now hard dick ready for penetration. He effortlessly slides on a condom, and dives into her wet, throbbing treasure-trove. She continues to moan and shake, as Harold fucks her hard and steady. She screams as he rails her. She loves every rough intense moment of it.

"Do you like the way I'm fucking your sweet pussy?" He questions in an overtly dominating tone.

"Hell yeah! Fuck this pussy Daddy!" She responds, completely enjoying the moment. He continues banging her walls with reckless abandonment. She groans, howls, and grips the sheets, as if possessed by a legion of demons. He gives her a few more heavy concentrated thrusts, and they both reach the top of the mountain.

"Oh fuck Daddy, thank you!" She releases in a breathy, shaky voice.

"No thank you." Harold responds as he slides out of her. They are both satisfied with having their physical needs met. Harold wipes the sweat from off of his forehead, and goes into the bathroom for a quick clean up before heading home.

9:12pm: Harold walks out of the apartment building. Malcolm on the verge of dosing off, quickly shakes off the drowsiness, and fumbles to get his recording device running. He successfully gets most of Harold's journey from the apartment to his car. Considering the quietness of the parking lot, he waits until Harold begins driving before starting up his car.

9:49pm: Harold pulls into his driveway, powers off his second cell phone, and stashes it before going into the house. He is happy and relaxed. Vicki was exactly what he needed to clear the space in his complicated mess of a mind. He contemplates calling Amanda before stepping inside, but decides that it would better if he waited until tomorrow.

DAY 4

9:05am: After settling in for another day at the office, Harold receives a call on his second cell phone.

"Hey baby, I can't wait to see you today." Amanda says in a happy upbeat tone.

"I was just about to call you. Are you still at the motel?" He asks as he checks through as series of urgent emails.

"Well, right now I'm at work, but I'll be staying at Alicia's house until next week. I'm going to pick up all of my stuff from the house tomorrow."

"So how did Carl take it?"

"Well, I don't really know. I haven't talked to him since I broke it off. I called him this morning, but he didn't answer."

"Okay...so what do you think is going on with him, you don't think he tried to kill himself do you?" Even though he has taken Carl's wife, Harold still has no ill will towards him, especially considering the complexity of their situation.

"I doubt it. I've never known him to be the suicidal type, even when things weren't going right. You've known him longer than me, so I should be asking you that question instead."

"Well, I mean…yeah, you do have a point." Harold's conscience really starts to fuck with him, as he thinks about his broken relationship with Carl. A spike of remorse resounds deep inside of him. He knows that his status and financial stability, have contributed greatly to his lack of consideration for others. He has second thoughts, in regards to what he is about to tell Amanda. He is about to make major choices that will greatly affect her life, as well as his own. "Okay, umm let's not think about that anymore, it's only going to cloud our judgment, and hinder us from finding true happiness. I have a lot of things that I need to discuss and come clean to you about, so what time do you go to lunch today?" Harold is ready to disclose his fling with Vicki, and announce his plans of Amanda and himself getting their own place together.

"I go to lunch at twelve, but I can probably sneak out ten minutes earlier. Did you want to meet up?"

"Yes, I really need to tell you what's on my mind." Harold says as he feels a huge weight starting to lift from off of his shoulders.

"Okay baby, I'll be there at twelve on the dot." Amanda responds before the call ends. The wheels are in motion; now the next thing on Harold's agenda is to break it off with Vicki.

11:59am: Amanda pulls up in front of Harold office. Like clockwork, Harold emerges from the building. He quickly hops in her car, and they head off. Malcolm has decided that after today, he should have enough evidence for Spellman to present to Denise. Even though he does not have actual footage of Harold engaging in sexual acts, he still has enough to make a flawless argument in a divorce proceeding. As usual, he follows the sorry excuse for a man.

12:11pm: Amanda and Harold arrive at a different destination than their previous outings. They arrive at sandwich-based bar and grill called Pappy's Bread. Once inside, they take a small table close to a series of large windows. They are in perfect view for filming. Malcolm seizes the opportunity and immediately begins recording.

"So what did you want to tell me?" Amanda inquires as she glosses over the lunch menu. Harold pauses and thinks before speaking. He has a lot to say, and does not want any part of it to be misconstrued.

"Well, I already told you that I'm leaving my wife, and I've decided to break the news to her tonight. In addition to breaking the news to Denise, I also have to break it off with a fling I was seeing while you were still with Carl. I don't have anything serious with the person, but if we're going to start our situation off right; I have to tell you everything. I want us to start with a clean slate. Amanda baby, what I feel with you is something that I've never felt before. The feeling that I have in my heart, is something that I need to keep feeling. I don't want it to go away, and I don't want you to go away. What I'm saying is that, I want to get serious with you. Oh, and I want us to have our own place together." Harold's announcements, have Amanda completely floored. She doesn't know how to respond. The news is bittersweet. She ecstatic about

Harold being ready to have an official relationship; but at the same, she is upset with the fact that he has been having a fling outside of his marriage and their relationship. A small inkling of doubt starts to form in her rational mind.

"Wait, so you mean to tell me that you have someone else besides Denise and me?"

"Well yes but, it's not what you think. As of today, I'm through with her, and every other woman but you!"

"Okay that sounds good and all, but how can I trust what you're saying? I mean I know that I should be the last person to have doubts considering my own situation, but how do I know that you won't do the same thing to me somewhere down the line?" Amanda questions as she continues looking over the menu. Harold understands her reservations, and thinks of a way to properly put her mind at ease.

As Harold is thinking of the perfect choice of words, a waitress approaches their table. She is a petite light skinned female with sandy brown hair. Her bubbly demeanor instantly catches their attention

"Hello folks. How are ya'll doing? My name is Cassie, and I'll be your server for today. What can I start you guys off with, any drinks or appetizers?" Cassie asks in a warm perky manner.

"Hi Cassie, I would like the Soup and bread lunch special with a small Pepsi." Amanda says while scanning over the young vibrant girl.

"Okay, and what type of soup and side salad would you like?"

"Umm, give me the Chicken Soup Surprise and a Caesar salad."

"Alright, and what would you like sir?" Harold quickly scans the menu and picks the first thing that catches his eye.

"Uh, give me the Roast Beef French Dip, with a small Greek salad." He murmurs as he second-guesses his decision of divulging his fling.

"Alright let me take these menus, and I'll be back in a few with your lunch choices." Cassie says before heading off towards the kitchen.

"Okay so let me get this straight, I give you what you want, and now you're having reservations about us, are you serious?" Harold exclaims while trying to keep his voice from elevating.

"Harold, I just need to know that we're going to have something different from what we're both walking away from. I want to be the only one that gets your heart and great sex from here on out! I'm not sharing you, and once we take this step, there is no turning back!" Amanda's words are stern and have a deathly seriousness to them. Harold now realizes just how invested she is to the notion of them being a couple.

"Babes, you have my absolute word that from this day forward, it's just you and I. No one else will ever come between us. I'm done with cheating! The way that you make me feel is different from anything I've ever known. Even Denise has never made me feel like this. I don't care if our families have objections about us being together. I don't care if I lose friends because of it. Amanda honey, all I care about is you, and your happiness!" Harold lets his emotions pour out of his mouth like water breaking free from a dam. He means every word, every syllable; he has truly found love. Harold's declaration has erased all doubt from Amanda's consciousness. She feels the sincerity in each word. She is ready to be happy, and run off with her true love. She is ready to have an ending like the fairytales she obsessed over as a child. Her knight in flawed armor has slain the dragon, and rescued her heart. Amanda, energized by the love, reaches over and steals a quick kiss from Harold. Malcolm, who is still recording, captures it perfectly through the huge front window.

12:47pm: Amanda and Harold arrive back at Harold's office. They kiss and say their goodbyes, before Harold exits the vehicle. Once out of the car, he watches as Amanda's car heads off. He then takes a quick glance at his surroundings, and notices a man that appears to be filming him! Malcolm, realizing that Harold is aware of his presence, gets out of his car and acts as if he's capturing images of the entire street. Harold stares intensely at Malcolm as the gears in his head start working. He knows that he's seen the man before, but he can't quite put his finger on where. He contemplates confronting him, but doesn't want to seem like some sort of paranoid wacko. Malcolm continues his impromptu performance. He stays calm, and avoids eye contact with Harold. After a few moments of indecisiveness, Harold chooses to confront him. Malcolm takes notice of Harold walking towards him, and a similar incident comes to mind. He stays calm and prepares for the confrontation.

"Excuse me, what are you doing?" Harold inquires in an interrogative manner as he gives Malcolm a stone hard look.

"Uh, what are you talking about?" Malcolm plays dumb and gives Harold a blank stare.

"Dude, why are you following me?" Harold's inquiry puts Malcolm on the defense.

"Following you? Why would I be following you? I don't even know who you are!" Malcolm says with a defensive tone in his voice.

"You were following and filming me!" Harold exclaims as his anger starts to build.

"Look fella, I don't know what you're talking about. I'm an artist. I capture real images and turn them into unique pieces of art, using a combination of various software programs, and real time texture paints." Malcolm has used this cover so many times, that he has mastered it from every single angle.

"Okay so if you're an artist, you should have samples of your work available for the public to view, am I right?"

"Oh I do" Malcolm responds as he reaches in his pocket and pulls out a mock business card "Here's my website," He says as he hands Harold the card. "Go on there, and check out my stuff."

Harold reads the card, and is at a loss for words. He is so embarrassed. Images from his childhood come to mind, images of Bugs Bunny morphing into a Jackass during a moment of stupidity. Harold feels the blood rush to his cheeks. He feels like a Jackass indeed.

"Umm, okay. I will check em' out. Sorry about that…" He utters before making a hasty retreat. Malcolm has had enough narrow escapes in his time of being a private investigator, to know when to wrap it up. He quickly returns to his vehicle, and calls up attorney Spellman. Spellman's secretary answers.

"Spellman and associates, Linda speaking, how may I help you?"

"Hey Linda, its Malcolm Scott, I need to speak with Spellman, tell him it's urgent."

"Okay, I'm transferring you right now." Linda says before transferring the call.

"Attorney Spellman speaking,"

"Hey Spellman, its Malcolm, I'm done."

"Are you sure that you have enough on the guy?"

"Yeah, I'm positive. With the footage and pictures that I have, your case against that creep will be foolproof!"

"Sounds great, how about you swing by my office in like the next forty minutes, I'll be ready for you by then."

"Alright I gotcha"

Malcolm arrives at Spellman's office. He is both excited and relieved to be finished with the mess of Harold. The past few days have taken a toll on him. He is both repulsed, and in awe of Harold's activeness. He ponders how such a person could be so active, and manage not to crash and burn. He has not dealt with something as intense and all consuming in years; he's drained both mentally and physically. The bags under his eyes, and the slight red tint of the eyes themselves, are telltale signs of sleep deprivation. Now that his task is completed, a long week of rest, awaits him. Thanks to the considerable amount of money Spellman paid to retain his services, a week length vacation, is now feasible.

Spellman sits in his office awaiting the meeting with Malcolm. He is anxious to see the evidence that Malcolm has complied. He loves righting wrongs and adding more money to his already abundant bank account. He has certainly carved out a niche by effectively providing legal representation, to high society's unhappily married. His last case alone, netted him twenty-five percent of a multimillion-dollar divorce settlement. Thanks to lack of self-control on the part of the wealthy, his years of law school have paid off quite handsomely. Spellman takes notice of his office line flashing, and picks up. "Mr. Spellman, Malcolm is here to see you."

"Okay thank you, send him back." Spellman is giddy with anticipation. His anticipation is comparable to that of a child waiting to open a birthday gift. A knock on the door lets him know that Malcolm has arrived. "Come in," Malcolm enters the room with evidence in hand. "Hello Malcolm, have a seat." Spellman greets his weary guest and gets right down to business.

"Okay here it goes," Malcolm says as he starts up one of the video files. Spellman's eyes light up as he watches the undisputable footage. Thoughts of another victory flash in his head.

"Wow this guy really has quite the sexual appetite." Spellman murmurs as he continues to watch the videos

"Yeah, I got exhausted just filming it." Malcolm retorts.

"I don't know how he's managed not to get caught."

"He's probably been doing it so long, that he knows exactly what not to do." Harold's abundance in extramarital activity, will make for one of the most exciting cases that Spellman has had privy to in years "This is good stuff, what about the photos?" Spellman asks, evidently pleased with the videos.

"Oh yeah those are pretty good too." Malcolm utters before setting up his photo gallery. "Check em' out"

The photo gallery shows Harold in various compromising situations, from kissing in Amanda's car, to going in and out of Vicki's apartment.

"Okay, well I think we definitely have enough to win the case and get a sizeable settlement. Thank you for your remarkable service. I will definitely do business with you in the future." Spellman shakes Malcolm's hand, and shows him out. Once Malcolm has left, Spellman places a call to Denise Atkins.

Denise, in the middle of watching an episode of Judge Judy, answers the call. "Hello"

"Hello Mrs. Atkins, this is attorney Spellman. I have something that you definitely need to see. How soon can you make it down to my office?"

"Umm…well I can make it down after my girls get home from school." Denise feels a sense of dread creeping over her. She knows that the lawyer has something that will give truth to her intuition.

"Okay great, I will see then."

"Okay" she murmurs as a terrible, sinking feeling begins to form in the pit of her gut. The phrase "Be careful what you wish for because you just might get it" echoes in her head.

Denise parks outside of the office of Spellman and associates. She has second thoughts about going through with it. She doesn't want to know, but she needs to know. She needs to know the truth about Harold. She forces herself out of the car. Her legs feel as heavy as lead, and her heartbeat is as fast as the fluttering wings of a hummingbird. The closer she gets, the more intense her panic sensations become. She pushes on and manages to make it inside, once inside the drab typical looking Attorney's office, her panic symptoms peak. She can barely get out her words as she reaches the receptionist desk. "Uh…hi…I-I'm here to see attorney Spellman."

"Okay and you are?"

"Denise, Denise Atkins"

"Alright Denise, have a seat and I will let attorney Spellman know that you're here to see him." Linda pages Spellman. "Hello Mr. Spellman, Denise Atkins is here to see you"

"Okay Linda, send her back"

"Mr. Spellman is ready to see you Mrs. Atkins"

"Thank you" Denise responds before making her way to Spellman's office. She reaches Spellman's office, and softly knocks on the door.

"Come in" Spellman says in a slightly elevated tone. Denise enters the office and takes a seat. Attorney Spellman greets her and immediately shows her the evidence. Denise's heart breaks as she views the incriminating evidence. She feels sick to her stomach while watching her Husband, kiss and grope other women. She almost loses it completely when he walks into Vicki's apartment building.

"Th-That's enough, I don't want to see anymore," she utters as she holds her mouth and she turns away. She fights back her tears and struggles to keep her composure. She feels numb. It feels like someone has just died. Her hands start to shake uncontrollably as she rises from her seat.

"Are you okay?" Spellman asks in a concerned tone.

"Yeah, I'm okay. I think I've seen enough, you can shut it off now." Spellman closes the programs. "I will let you know when I'm ready to move forward." She says before abruptly rushing out of his office. Denise power walks out of his office. She continues the hurried pace until she reaches her car. Tears run down her face as she starts up the engine. Her world is crashing down around her. She realizes that she has wasted precious amounts of love and devotion, on a doomed marriage. Never in a million years would she have thought that the man, in whom she gave her best years to, would end up being the cause of so much heartache. She completely falls to pieces as her car sits with its engine idling. She shuts out the world around her as she releases all of the dark feelings of misery and despair. She finishes her moment of release and realizes what she must now do. She realizes that he must leave; he has to go! She does not want that type of man setting a horrible example for her precious girls.

Harold is in the middle of a conference call when he receives a text message from Vicki *"Still thinking about last night…* ☺ *Call me when you get a chance sexy xoxo."* He contemplates texting her back and breaking the news. He finishes handling business, and opts to call her instead.

"Hello sexy." Vicki answers in her sweetest, most seductive voice.

"Hey Vicki…uh listen… about last night…"

"Yeah it was great! I need you to give it to me like that more often."

"Well, what I called to tell you is that there isn't going to be anymore nights like last night. Vicki we're done." Harold murmurs with sincerity.

"What? We're done, what do you mean we're done?" The tone in Vicki's voice changes drastically.

"I mean that I can't do this anymore. The way things went at dinner last night, really made me realize that we're not meant for each other, and believe me, it's not you, it's completely me, I'm set in my ways. And…."

"Oh so instead of telling me yesterday during diner, you decide to get one last fuck and then dump me? You're a piece of shit! My sister told me not fuck with your white ass! She told me you wasn't about shit! I should've listened! You're a sorry ass muthafucka, and I hope you get yours. I hope you get everything that's coming to you! You dirty bastard!" Vicki ends the call before Harold can respond. He expected it to go sour. It's not the first time he's had to do it, but he wants to make sure it will be his last. He takes the prepaid phone, and hurls it across the room. It hits the wall and shatters. Just as he promised Amanda, he is done.

Harold arrives home from work. He steps into the house expecting his little angel to come running, but gets a hard slap to the face instead. He recoils from the impact. It completely catches him off guard "WHAT THE FUCK!" He yells as he rubs the side of his stinging face. Denise stands before him. Her eyes are blood shot red; she reeks of alcohol and smoke! Her light brunette tendrils are a disheveled mess.

"So you couldn't be man enough to tell me? You had to string me along and waste my time, waste years of my precious life! Why weren't you man enough to do the right thing?"

"What the hell are you talking about?"

"You know exactly what I'm talking about, the young black girl and Carl's wife! That's what the fuck I'm talking about!"

Denise's searing words leave Harold speechless. He wonders how she found out about Amanda and Vicki. He also wonders if she has found out about any of his other past flings.

"Whoa, calm down. It's definitely not what you think…"

"Well, you know what I think; I think that you're a lying worthless piece of shit that deserves to never see MY DAUGHTERS AGAIN!"

"Hold on one fucking minute, they're my girls too! And you can't keep me away from them, and…"

"LIKE HELL I CAN'T! ONCE THE COURT SEES ALL OF YOUR EXTRAMARITAL ACTIVITES, I'M PRETTY SURE THAT THEY WILL AGREE WITH MY DECISION!" Denise's words instantly make Harold think back to his weird meeting earlier.

"That motherfucker was filming me!" He mumbles as he mentally connects the pieces of the puzzle. He knows that he has royally fucked up. He tries to think of something to say that will neutralize the situation, but his mind draws a blank.

"I know about everything, so you need to finally man up, and accept the consequences of your actions. I'm done, see you in court!" Denise walks out of the house and leaves Harold alone to stew in his own misery.

After sulking for a few, he decides to call Amanda. "Hey Amanda"

"Harold? Why are you calling me from a different number? I've been calling your phone like crazy and it kept going to voicemail."

"I got rid of it. It's done; I'm ready to start our new life."

"So you broke it off with your fling, and you told Denise?"

"Yeah, it's all out in the open, no more sneaking around, and no more lies. Look, I really need to see you, are you still at Alicia's?"

"Yes, but I don't think it would be a good I idea for you to come over here. Carl came by earlier, and we had to call to police. He's really out of it. I don't feel safe anymore."

"Okay, so what do you propose we do? It's definitely not a good idea for you to come here"

"Umm how about we meet at that Super 8?"

"Well actually, I've got a better place in mind."

Amanda pulls up to The Ritz Carlton. She smiles as she thinks about seeing Harold. She is so preoccupied with seeing her love that she fails to notice Carl's car slowly creep from around the corner. He watches as his wife goes inside of the swanky hotel. Amanda is bursting with excitement as she makes her way inside. Harold is all hers. They are officially a couple. She gushes with joy as she steps onto the elevator. She envisions them spending future days together. She reminisces about being in his strong toned arms. She fantasizes about staring into his striking, breathtaking eyes. She throbs as she thinks about his love going inside of her. She feels bad for Denise, but is relieved that after this night, they will no longer have to sneak around. Once she reaches her floor, Amanda calls Harold. "Hi baby, I'm here"

"Okay honey, I'm waiting for you" Harold responds as he rises from off of the bed. He is surprised that he managed to dose off without being aware of it. He grabs a mint from off of the nightstand, and pops it into his mouth to chase away the odor of sleep. Before Amanda can knock, Harold opens the door. "I missed you," he says before grabbing his woman and giving her a strong passionate kiss. Amanda melts in his strong embrace. She's been waiting all day for this moment. They quickly remove their clothing, and engage. Harold penetrates Amanda's throbbing moist womanhood, and she purposely digs her nails into his back. She's wanted to do it for so long, and now she is taking full advantage of their exclusivity. She claws and bites his flesh, in approval of his sexual labor, and for the first time, they make guiltless love. They are free from everything, and free to give their all to one another. They engage in one of the rawest, most unadulterated forms of sex. Their sex is explosively primal. Every thrust, every moan, every scratch, every bite is uninhibited. Amanda melts in love as Harold thrusts his frustrations away. They continue to go at it as time slips by, and evening gives way to the night.

Now lying in the Aftermath of hot fulfilling intercourse, they stare into each other's eyes, gaze into each other's souls. They communicate without words. Harold and Amanda are completely satisfied. After some time, Harold interrupts their silent communication with a soft sincere declaration. "I want this feeling forever, I want you forever…"

DAY 5

9:02am: Harold wakes up with Amanda nestled close to him. Her warm body feels perfect up against his naked flesh. His nose takes in her sweet womanly fragrance as he glances at the rays of sunlight touching her soft exposed skin. He thinks about their future together. In spite of their obstacles with Carl and Denise, he looks forward to making a life with her, he knows that Denise is going to give him hell, but does not quite know what trouble Carl is capable of causing.

He feels terrible about the way things went with Denise. He wishes things would have went differently with her. She deserved better. He knows that if not for her seeing evidence of his infidelity, things would've definitely went better; if his hand had not been forced, he could've easy defused the hostility. He would've handled it by doing what he has always done in those instances. He would've smooth talked her into a calm docile state, and then broke the news in a civil manner. He contemplates hiring a full time person to oversee his company's day-to-day operations, and devoting more time to his personal life. He knows that with his imminent divorce on the horizon, he's going to have to keep it running smoothly so he can afford to pay lawyer fees, child support, and in a worst case scenario, alimony. Seeing as how a sizable amount of his time and attention will be devoted to the messy debacles of divorce and custody cases, he is definitely going to need someone else's clear mind to oversee it.

He shifts his attention back to the object of his affection. Amanda is everything that he has ever wanted in a woman. For the first time in his life, he feels completely satisfied. "Sorry Carl" He mumbles as he thinks about his victory. He feels bad considering how close they once were, but it's hard to have control over whom you fall in love with. If there is a God somewhere, Harold knows that the omnipresent entity is probably not too pleased with him. "Wake up sleepy head" Harold mumbles as he gently strokes Amanda's hair. She rouses and is delighted to find herself next to him

"Hey Papi, mmm last night was great." She murmurs before getting a brief stretch in. "You always know how to please me."

"I wouldn't be your man if didn't. I don't mean to put a damper on the mood that you're in, but I would really like to know what happen with Carl yesterday."

"It's cool. As good I'm feeling right now, it'll take a lot more than that to get me down. Anyway, he pulled up outside of Alicia's house with his radio blasting the same song repeatedly it was creepy. He got out of the car and just stood there staring at me. I couldn't tell if he was drunk or high, but I knew that something wasn't right about him. I looked up the song afterwards; the song is "Never Gonna Give You Up" by some old soul singer named Jerry "The Iceman" Butler.

"Oh wow really?" Harold blurts as he listens to her story.

"Yeah, and up to that point, I had never heard that song before. I wanted to confront him, and get him to stop playing that creepy song, but I was terrified of him!"

"So how did the cops get involved? I mean what else did he do other than play the music?"

"He didn't do anything else, but after hearing the song for a fifth time, Alicia couldn't take it anymore. She's the one that ended up calling the cops. She started yelling at him, telling him that the cops were on their way and if he knew what was good for him, he would leave! After playing the song two more times, he slowly got back in the car and left. It was disturbing. I think he's gone off the deep end. I'm having second thoughts about getting my things from the house. I might need a police escort!"

"Don't worry babes, if worse come to worse, I'll hire some movers and personally see to it that nothing happens to you, or your things."

"Thanks Babes,"

"You're welcome, so have you been looking at some places for us?"

"Yeah, I found a few I liked. I scheduled some appointments for next week."

"Okay good, well enough with all of this seriousness, how about we get a quickie in before checkout time?"

"You read my mind stallion" Amanda responds as she grabs his semi-erect cock. The two begin to kiss and grope in between the soft high thread count, Egyptian cotton sheets. Amanda scoots down and begins servicing Harold. He watches as the sheet covering her head goes up and down over his now erect manhood. Her warm wet mouth deeply engulfs him. He lets out a low manly groan as she passionately blows his mind with her oral precision. Once she is done, she positions herself on top of him. Harold's hard penis plunges into her wetness. She moans as it penetrates her. She begins rhythmically riding his firm pleasure stick. Harold grabs her curves as her walls stroke his stiff penis. He likes to be in control, so he smoothly flips her over and takes charge. He slowly grinds her insides, as he kisses her neck. She loves the way his lips feel as they press up against her soft golden skin. Their romp extends past the quickie limit and crosses over into a full session. Hot sex has just turned into full on lovemaking. Harold continues pumping her soft box, until she climatically releases in a violent explosion of seizure-like proportions. Harold, so caught up in the moment, releases his hot fluid inside of her. They are completely enamored with each other.

"Oh fuck baby! That was incredible!" She exclaims while still shaking.

"Yeah, it's always great between us. I'm about to hop in the shower. Why don't you come and join me."

"Okay as soon as I stop shaking." she shoots back. Harold smiles in approval. He grabs his things, and heads into the bathroom. After a few moments of rest, Amanda regains her composure and begins to gather all of her belongings. While gathering her things, a strong feeling of trepidation overtakes her. It is a very intense feeling, unlike anything she has ever experienced before. The feeling is very negative, devoid of hope. She struggles to shake it off, but it refuses to leave. She makes it into the bathroom with Harold, and it becomes more pronounced. "Hey baby I'm coming in." Amanda says in a forced bubbly tone, as she places her stuff on the bathroom counter. She steps into the warm steamy, shower. Harold turns to face her. He has a somewhat grim expression.

Unbeknownst to Amanda, Harold has an uneasy feeling as well. He wonders if his guilt getting the best of him, or if it's just a reaction to being under stress. "Is everything alright?" They ask each other in unison. It freaks them both out. They laugh and try to ignore the feelings. The laughter helps to reduce the bad vibes. In slightly better spirits, the two kiss and caress each other briefly before Harold gets out, and Amanda starts to wash up. Once dressed, Harold answers a call from his office. As he finishes his call, Amanda emerges from the bathroom.

"Hey baby, I really have to get out of here. I have to handle a few things at the office." Harold states before grabbing his things, and giving her a quick peck. Amanda dries off and follows suit.

As she steps in the elevator, the dreadful sensation resumes. She tries to rationalize the cause of it. She mentally goes over all of the less than great things going on in her life. The only thing that really sticks out is Carl. Her mind stays fixated on him as she reaches the lobby.

Once she gets outside, something else steals her attention. A quick glance at her car has revealed a new addition. There is something stuck underneath one of her windshield wipers. At first, she mistakes it for a parking ticket; but as she gets closer, she realizes that it is an envelope. She quickly scans the area as she grabs it from off the windshield. She gets in the car, opens the envelope, and gasps as she views the contents. The contents are pictures of her and Harold! She sees Harold start to pull off, and tries frantically to get his attention. Her attempts are unsuccessful, she calls his phone, and it goes straight to voicemail. She calls it several more times, but to no avail. She immediately starts up her car and tries to catch up with him. She manages to get within a few cars distance. She tries one last time to reach him by phone. Again, it goes to voicemail. "Harold baby, I need you to call back right away!" She blurts into the phone as panic sweeps over her.

Thinking about Amanda, Harold grabs his phone from out of his pocket. He tries to use it, but is unsuccessful; the battery has died. "Damn" he mumbles as he takes out his car charger. He plugs it up, and focuses back on the road. Preoccupied with a reckless driver in front of him, he fails to notice Amanda's vehicle five cars behind. He makes the corner just as the light turns red; leaving Amanda and the rest of the vehicles stuck at the light.

As he is driving, he realizes that he forgot some paperwork at the house. He decides to make a quick stop home before heading into the office.

11:32am: Harold arrives at his office. He pulls into the parking garage. He notices Amanda's car parked in his reserved parking spot. "What the fuck?" He questions as he stops in front of it. He gets out of the car and hears an old RnB song emanating from inside of her vehicle. It instantly makes him recall the situation that she told him about earlier. "Never gonna give you up..." He mumbles along with the soul singer as he walks toward her car. As he gets closer, he sees someone is sitting in the driver's seat. He reaches the driver's side, and sees Amanda's bloody lifeless body. Her throat has a large slash from ear to ear, and the handle of a knife is protruding from her gaped open mouth. "Oh sh..." before Harold can finish his thought, the sound of a gunshot echoes through the garage. Subsequently after, Harold feels a sharp sting in his lower abdomen. He looks down, and sees a hole with crimson liquid oozing out of it. He instantly goes into shock.

He turns, and sees Carl walking toward him with a smoking gun aimed in his direction. Harold feels his bladder emptying its urine contents as Carl fire two more shots at point blank range. Both shots hit Harold in the Chest. He falls backwards onto the floor of the garage. He feels a massive pain in his chest as he begins to shake uncontrollably. He starts to get dizzy. He manages to focus his vision, and sees Carl standing over him.

"You just had to ruin my life huh? You just had to take everything from me! You couldn't be happy with your family and all of your money! You just had to have her! How could do this to me, twice! I should've known it was you the first time! I should've known that it wasn't one of your employees. The coincidence hit too close to home! You were supposed to be my family! I loved you!" Tears run from Carl's eyes as he stands over his bleeding cousin, childhood memories of them playing together, flash in his head as he looks down at Harold. The memories make Carl's burning rage slowly dissipate, and become replaced by a deep sadness. "You knew how much I loved her, you heartless son of a bitch! I hope it was worth it, I'll see you in hell!" Carl puts the barrel of the gun in his mouth and pulls the trigger.

COMING IN FEBRUARY!

Leave Me Alone

A.D. Phillips

Library of Congress Cataloging-In-Publication Data is on file at the Library of Congress, Washington, DC.

Printed in the United States of America

For Tonia, My Loving Wife
The one that helped me get on the right track

Acknowledgements

Thanks to My wife Tonia, Mom, Dad, Alicia, Anthony, Aaliyah, Alexandria, Reggie, Sierra, Miles, and Javon

Tonia - Tolerated my addiction to success and helped me get on the right track

Mom – Always believed in me, even when I didn't.

Dad – Gave me the inspiration to seek something better than working a sucky job

Alicia - For believing in your big brother

Anthony, Aaliyah, and Alexandria – Gave me the need to get to a higher level.

Reggie, Sierra, and Miles – Accepted me into the fold.

Javon – For providing radio promotion and insight

Chapter 14

I WAKE UP and immediately begin thinking about what I have to do today. Becky slumbers peacefully next to me. Seeing her gives me confidence. I hope it doesn't hurt Lissa. I hope for the best as I get up and get ready to face the day. I know it's supposed to be wrong, but why don't I feel guilty? How can I just continue doing what I'm doing and not feel remorse? Am I crazy? Am I losing my mind? I love fucking and hanging out with both of them. What will her mother and Ashley think about this situation, and why don't I really give a fuck, or do I? I've gone too far to turn back now. Lissa will be here in the next few hours and I have to lay it on the line. I refuse to live a lie. I'm not going to be one of those guys who have to constantly lie and keep up a juggling act, so I'm just going to do it.

I get into the shower. It wakes up all of my senses. I feel my pores open up. The rushing water helps to clear my mind. It relaxes me. A voice in the distance interrupts my moment of tranquility. I hear the voice again. It sounds like one I've heard before, but I can't recall from where. I shut of the water and wait in silence to hear it again. After a few moments of being lost in anticipation, I hear it again. It sounds like someone calling my name, not my first name, my middle name. The voice is faint. I wrap a towel around my waist and slowly make my way out of the bathroom. I creep past the bedroom and see Becky still asleep in bed. Knowing it's not her, sends a sense of dread coursing throughout my body. I feel the adrenaline building up as my heart beat increases. I go from room to room expecting, or rather hoping to see someone, to prove my sanity to myself. I manage to make my way to the basement, and not find a single thing! As I make my way back upstairs, I see Becky at the top of the stairs.

"Hey Teddy I was looking for you, I was trying to see if you turned down the heat."

"No I didn't turn down the heat. I just got out of the shower."

"Well when I woke up, it was freezing cold in the bedroom."

"I don't know why it's so cold up there; the temperature is on seventy-six. I noticed it on the way back up from the basement." I go into the bedroom to feel it for myself. I enter the room and immediately notice the drastic difference in temperature. The bedroom is so cold that I can see my breath. I step back out into the hallway and the temperature is warm! Something is very wrong. I rush back into the room and grab my phone. I dash back out and punch in my code to check the surveillance footage. I look at footage from the time I leave the room until the time Becky wakes up. At first, I think it is something messing up on the footage, but as I continue to look, I notice that what I'm seeing isn't a glitch in the footage. What I'm seeing is what appears to be a shadowy silhouette. The way it moves is similar to that of a person. It moves around the whole room. It looks like it's searching for something. I see it leave out of the room. I switch the camera footage to the hallway camera. I spot the figure move down the hallway. The figure vanishes seconds before I see myself emerge out of the bathroom and creep past the bedroom. I put two & two together, and assume that the shadow man was probably the one calling out for Michael.

"Damn" Becky says as she glances over my shoulder at the footage.

"You know you could've asked to see it instead of standing on your tip toes" I say as I acknowledge her presence.

"I'm sorry baby it's a habit I guess" she responds.

"So what do you think it is?"

"Umm it looks like one of those shadow people from off of those ghost shows."

"You are really serious about this ghost stuff huh?"

"I'm just saying Teddy; most of the evidence points to it so what else could it be?"

"Okay well I will deal with that after we deal with Lissa."

"Fair enough, you're lucky that I don't scare easy, or I would've stopped coming by and staying over."

"I know baby, I recognize you female cojenes." I say before

planting a kiss on her soft sweet lips.

"Now jump in the shower and get ready for breakfast. Chef Teddy is serving up his world famous omelet!"

The sound of the doorbell echoes through the house as we finish eating breakfast.

"Lissa came earlier than I expected" I state before putting my fork down on my nearly finished plate. I slowly walk to the door, the whole time I'm fighting myself, trying to shake the fear that is starting to bubble inside of my being. I pause, take a deep breath, click the locks, and twist the knob. The door opens to reveal Lissa with a warm bubbly smile. I guess the signs of pregnancy must be true, because she appears to have a glow about her. "Come in" I say as I take her coat and get her seated. I want to beat around the bush, but something inside urges me to get straight to the point.

"Lissa I have something to tell you" I blurt out as I think of the next thing to say. Right as I'm about to continue speaking, Becky enters into the room.

"What the fuck is she doing here?" Lissa expels in a heated tone from out of her mouth. Becky responds before I can.

"I'm here because I need to be. There is no need to be hostile; I

6

have no problem with you. Actually, I like you." Becky smiles
before continuing to speak. "We all need to sit down and discuss a
few things."

"Teddy, what's going on?" Lissa questions me with a puzzled
expression on her face.

"Well Lissa, things are different now. I know that we're having
a baby, but I am involved with Becky as well" I feel a huge weight
being lifted as I release the information, Lissa's jaw drops as her
face freezes in disbelief.

"We're expecting as well." Becky chimes in as she grabs my
arm and stands next to me. Lissa quickly gets up. She puts her
hands on her hips, pauses for a moment, and looks down.

"So let me get this right, you called me over here not to show
me how much you love me, or even to show how much you've
missed me; you called me over here to tell me that you and this
tramp," She pauses and points at Becky "Are fucking and now
you're having a baby with her too! I knew there was something
going on between ya'll since I first saw her with you at the

7

hospital! I can't believe I was so fucking stupid! Now I remember why we broke up, because you're no good for me. I always knew that your flirty ways would end up being the end of us!" Lissa rushes at me and delivers a swift hard openhanded blow to the side of my face. I feel my head turn as I quickly recover from the blow. I instinctively grab Lissa.

"CALM DOWN NOW!" I yell as I try to prevent her from delivering any more blows. I struggle to keep myself from using too much force. I don't want to risk hurting her or the baby. In an act of desperation, I involuntarily shove her back onto the couch. "CALM THE FUCK DOWN AND LISTEN!" I demand as I rub my stinging face. Lissa has an extremely crazed look in her eyes, like that of a wounded animal backed into a corner. I'm so heated and confused that I struggle mentally for the next thing to say. Becky steps forward and begins to speak…

"I'm not trying to take Teddy from you; I want to share him with you." She proclaims in a calm almost serene manner.

"Are you crazy? Do you really think I want to share anything with you?" Lissa questions with a reddened tear filled face.

I watch in disbelief as Becky slowly walks over to the couch, and calmly sits next to Lissa. She then attempts to embrace her. I'm expecting the worse to happen. I want to step in and stop her before anything happens. The mental images of a catfight erupting, only add to my worry. Lissa fights it at first, but then she surrenders to it. It's like watching a Lion tamer. Becky uses some weird unknown force to grab the proverbial bull by the horns. Lissa cries on her shoulder, while Becky gently rubs her hair and continues to hold her. Becky looks over at me, and motions me over to them. At first, I'm apprehensive, but I slowly find myself drawing closer. She grabs my arm and places it around herself; I cautiously place the other one around Lissa. We all hug for a few moments before Becky scoots over and I take a seat in between them.

"Teddy, what am I supposed to tell my Mom, what am I suppose to tell Ashley? Oh Mom well see Ted's other woman, Becky said that she doesn't mind sharing him; Ashley it's okay maybe you will find one like him too, SOMEBODY TO SHARE!" Lissa expresses her legitimate concerns.

"Why do you have to tell them anything? We are all adults. I mean no disrespect, but this is your life to live not theirs." I say with a confident, absolute tone. I look over at Becky and see her smiling ear to ear. "Basically, what I'm saying is that, I want you to move in. We can all live here and deal with this on our own. As adults, we can handle this on our own. We can show them how this can turn into a happy-ending. All I'm saying is, let's try something different." Lissa sits in silence as she thinks about what I have just said. Becky is giddy with delight. She appears to be enjoying every moment of it.

"Teddy, I'm not that kind of woman. I can't accept the fact that, the person I'm committed to, is openly cheating on me! I won't allow it!" Lissa gets up and grabs her coat. "I...I can't deal with this right now, I have to go." She says as she walks toward the front door.

"Lissa wait," I try to stop her.

"Ted we're done! Get out of my way, I'm ready to leave!" She proclaims as she shoves me out of the way. I make one last attempt to stop her.

"No, let her go she will be back" Becky says as she grabs my hand.

"I hope your right" I respond as I watch the love of my life walk out the door.

"Leave Me Alone" a 438 page novel by fiction writer A. D. Phillips is an Erotic, scary, and deeply engaging tale that emerges readers into the life of Halo Insurance employee, Theodore Rhodes. The closer he gets to finding out the truth, the more upside down his world is turned. In the midst of discovering the truth, he finds himself caught in the middle of a love triangle between the love of his life, and the flame of his desire. Which one will he choose, or will he choose them both? Find out this February with the rerelease of "Leave Me Alone", and "Leave Me Alone: Deluxe Edition"

Leave Me Alone is a story that will have you reading the book cover to cover and craving more!

Both editions will be available on Amazon.com, Kindle, Barns and Noble.com, and nook.

Also, visit www.adpbooks.com for more info on the author.

Follow A.D. Phillips on twitter and like him on Facebook

ABOUT THE AUTHOR

A.D. Phillips was born in Cleveland, Ohio 1980. This is his second book. He lives in Lakewood, Ohio with his wife, stepson, and cat. He is also a father of three, and a stepfather of two. Creating stories for others to enjoy, has become an all-consuming passion. He is deeply engrossed in his work as an author. Simply put, he loves what he does

Made in the USA
Charleston, SC
13 January 2013